Copyright © 1998 by Nord-Süd Verlag AG, Gossau Zürich, Switzerland
First published in Switzerland under the title *Die blinde Fee*
English translation copyright © 1998 by North-South Books Inc.

All rights reserved.
No part of this book may be reproduced or utilized in any form
or by any means, electronic or mechanical, including photocopying,
recording, or any information storage and retrieval system,
without permission in writing from the publisher.

First published in the United States, Great Britain, Canada,
Australia, and New Zealand in 1998 by North-South Books,
an imprint of Nord-Süd Verlag AG, Gossau Zürich, Switzerland.

Distributed in the United States by North-South Books Inc., New York.

Library of Congress Cataloging-in-Publication Data is available.
A CIP catalogue record for this book is available from The British Library.
ISBN 1-55858-970-8 (trade binding)
1 3 5 7 9 TB 10 8 6 4 2
ISBN 1-55858-973-2 (library binding)
1 3 5 7 9 LB 10 8 6 4 2
Printed in Belgium

The Blind Fairy

A tale by
BRIGITTE SCHÄR

with illustrations by
JULIA GUKOVA

Translated by J. Alison James

North South Books

NEW YORK · LONDON

In the middle of a distant land stood a dark and gloomy mountain. The people who lived there would have loved to move away. But where could they go? This was their home; the fields belonged to them.

As time went on, the mountain became ever more terrible. The people didn't know that up on the peak, in a palace, lived a blind fairy. Day after day she sat on her golden throne, dressed in the most beautiful clothes, waiting for someone to visit her.

"Is everything prepared?" asked the blind fairy.

Dwarves answered her, disguising their voices to sound like her old servants. "Yes," they said. "We have readied everything just as you wanted. Delicious food is cooked, the carpet is rolled out, the palace is scrubbed spotless. Everything gleams."

They made faces and grinned at one another.

"Well done, my dear servants," said the fairy. "Soon the people will come up to visit me."

She said this every day, but no one ever came.

"Tell me how the mountain looks," said the fairy.

"It is mighty," said the dwarves. "The mightiest mountain in the land. It is greener and more fertile than any other mountain. Everything on it grows and flourishes."

"And I see none of it," sighed the fairy. "How much I would give if only I could see it all again."

The dwarves grinned rudely. They had prepared nothing. Not today or any other day. Nobody would be invited. Nobody would come. The dwarves liked the dark, gloomy mountain just the way it was and did not want anything there to be beautiful again.

As usual, after sunset the
dwarves took the fairy to bed.

As soon as the fairy was asleep,
the dwarves turned night into day.
They crawled out of all the crannies
and caves. From everywhere around
they stormed to the palace. The wild
revels began.

The fairy was woken by the
terrible noise. How the thunderstorms
rage, she thought. The wind is whistling
so wildly through the palace that it
sounds like eerie music.

The fairy slept little, and was still tired when the dwarves came for her in the morning. "What terrible thunderclaps," she said. "I didn't sleep a wink."

"Yes," said the dwarves. "It was a terrible storm."

The fairy sighed. "Surely the wind from the storm has done great damage. Go down and help the people put their fields and houses back in order. You may send their children up here to me while you work."

The dwarves only laughed. They rollicked about wildly and made mischief all day long.

The fairy got ready without their help. She prepared everything for the children, feeling her way around the kitchen and through the rest of the palace. Again and again she stumbled over things lying in her path.

But the children did not come.

Perhaps they can't find me, thought the fairy, and she groped her way out to the balcony.

"Here I am, children," called the fairy. "Come along! I am here!" Then, quite clearly, she heard titters. That is the children, she thought joyfully. They are playing a game with me. They've hidden themselves, want me to find them.

"I can't see you. I can't see anything at all. I am blind," she called.

Again she heard the titters.

"Don't laugh at me," cried the fairy. "Come here to me!"

"You come to us!" she heard someone call.

There was nothing the blind fairy could do but grope her way outside the palace, where she had not set foot for so long. She stumbled down the steps. She bumped against a wall, fell down, picked herself up, tripped, and fell again. Finally she crawled along on all fours.

"Where are you? Give me a sign!"

Giggling came from all around.

"There are so many of you!" called the fairy excitedly. She stood up again and stumbled on down the mountain without finding anyone.

So the fairy managed to get down to the woods. She sat on the ground and breathed in the fresh air. These children have made a fool of me, she thought. And yet she felt quite happy.

At nightfall the fairy grew tired and lay down and went to sleep. No storm woke her this night. She slept soundly. In the morning she felt wonderfully rested. She groped her way from tree to tree. Suddenly she felt mossy stones.

"Here you are at last," said an ancient woman, emerging from a cave.

The fairy was startled. "Who are you?" she asked.

"Someone you don't know, but who knows you," she heard the voice say.

"Why don't I know you?" asked the fairy. "Why haven't you come to visit me in my palace, when you live so close by?"

"It wasn't possible," said the old woman. "The time had not yet come. But now you have come down yourself. That is good."

The woman and the fairy had much to tell each other.

"So the mountain isn't pleasant and fertile?" asked the fairy, shocked.

"It is barren beyond these woods," answered the old woman.

"And the people in the valley?" asked the fairy. "How is it for them?"

"They are afraid of the mountain more than anything else in the world," said the woman.

"But at least my palace is inviting, isn't it?" asked the fairy.

"It is a horrible, sinister, tumbledown castle," answered the old woman.

The fairy began to cry.

"Before I was blind, the palace was bright and beautiful," sobbed the fairy. "My servants were true to me. They would do anything for me."

"After you went blind," said the old woman, "dwarves came and chased away your servants. Since then the dwarves have reigned in a terrible way."

"Why have they let me go on living in the palace?" asked the fairy.

"Playing tricks on you was fun for them," said the woman.

"I never noticed any of this!" cried the fairy. "If I weren't blind, I would change everything."

Hardly had she said this than it seemed that she could see a little. Then she could see the old woman. She saw the trees, the sun, the sky. With tears in her eyes she thanked the old woman.

The woman answered, "If you hadn't forgotten you possessed the powers of a fairy, you would never have become blind. Now go, and set everything right again."

From way down the mountain, the fairy could hear the vile noise, the howling and screeching of the dwarves. She climbed higher and soon was so close that she could see everything too. How shocked she was. The palace was in ruins and overrun by thousands of dwarves.

The fairy wanted to flee. But then she thought of the old woman. "You can do it," she told herself.

The fairy climbed up the wide steps. When she stood at the top, she called out in a loud voice, "I have returned!"

For a moment, all was still.

"Be off with you!" she cried, enraged. "You are useless riffraff. Get out of my sight! Leave this mountain! Away from this land! I don't want to see any of you ever again!"

The dwarves laughed. "There are thousands of us. You are alone. What can you do against all of us?"

"You are dwarves," she declared, "but *I* am a fairy!"

And so she cast her magic spell.